PAWSOME PUPPY ADVENTURES!

A Random House PICTUREBACK® Book

Random House 🏠 New York

CONTENTS

RYDER

Whenever there's a problem in Adventure Bay, Ryder and his heroic team of pups, the PAW Patrol, are ready to help! There's no job too big and no pup too small.

"PAW Patrol to the Lookout!" shouts Ryder.

MARSHALL

"I'm all fired up!" says Marshall proudly.
Marshall is the team's brave Dalmatian fire dog.
He's always excited to race off on any ruff-ruff rescue, though
sometimes his excitement can make him
a little clumsy.

MARSHALL'S PUP HOUSE

transforms into a fire truck.
Inside his Pup Pack is a double-
spray fire hose.
    And no matter what happens,
Marshall has a happy, can-do
attitude!

CHASE

"Chase is on the case!" barks the PAW Patrol's smart, organized police pup, Chase.

Chase is the athletic leader of the pack. He's a German shepherd who likes to do things by the book. He can herd traffic, block off dangerous roads, and sniff out the solution to any mystery.

CHASE'S PUP HOUSE transforms into a police truck. His Pup Pack can provide him with a megaphone, a searchlight, a net, and other items that help his paws uphold the laws.

SKYE

"Pups away!" cheers Skye, the PAW Patrol's fearless daredevil.

This cockapoo pup is smaller than the other members of the team, but she never backs down from a challenge. She's ready to fly off on any adventure!

SKYE'S PUP HOUSE

is a trailer that turns into a helicopter. Her Pup Pack is filled with things that help her take to the sky.

She loves snowboarding, playing her Pup Pup Boogie dance game, and getting paw-dicures.

RUBBLE

"Rubble on the double!" barks Rubble, the team's tough construction pup. Strong, helpful, and friendly, this five-year-old bulldog loves to build and dig. He stays active with skateboarding and snowboarding, but when he gets dirty, he enjoys long, warm bubble baths.

RUBBLE'S PUP PACK

opens to reveal a bucket scoop. His Pup House becomes a digger with a bucket shovel.

Can you dig it? Rubble can!

ROCKY

"Green means go!" cheers Rocky, the PAW Patrol recycling pup.

This mixed breed is one creative canine. He can find treasure in someone else's trash and use it to solve nearly any problem! As Rocky always says, "Don't lose it—reuse it!"

ROCKY'S PUP PACK has all kinds of tools, including a big mechanical claw.

When he needs to hit the road, his Pup House becomes a recycling truck.

ZUMA

"Let's dive in!" shouts Zuma, the team's water-rescue dog.

Zuma is the youngest member of the team, a five-year-old Labrador who is full of energy. He loves all things water-related—from surfing to diving, and even bathing!

ZUMA'S PUP HOUSE

turns into a hovercraft, and his Pup Pack has air tanks and propellers to help him dive deep underwater.

"Ready, set, let's get wet!" says Zuma.

PAW PATROL IS READY TO ROLL!

"Whenever there's trouble, just yelp for help!" says Ryder.

It was the day of the Annual Mayor's Balloon Race, and Adventure Bay's own Mayor Goodway was nervous.

"Why did I ever agree to a balloon race?" she said, covering her eyes. "I have to get over my fear of heights."

"Don't worry. I'll be in the balloon to help you," said Ryder. "Ready to unroll the balloon, pups?"
"We're ready!" Rubble barked.

19

Rubble and Chase unrolled the dusty balloon.
"Uh-oh!" Chase said. "It's got a . . . a . . . *ACHOO!*"
When he had stopped sneezing from the dust, he
continued, ". . . a hole! A ripped balloon can't hold air!"

Mayor Goodway groaned. "Mayor Humdinger from Foggy Bottom will win again!"

"Don't worry," Ryder said. "We'll get this balloon ready for the race. No job is too big, no pup is too small."

Ryder pulled out his PupPad and called the rest of the PAW Patrol.

The PAW Patrol quickly assembled at the Lookout. "Ready for action, Ryder, sir!" Chase barked.

Ryder told the pups about the mayor's balloon. "We need to fix the balloon for the race. Rocky, can you find something in your recycling truck that we can use to patch it?"

"Don't lose it, reuse it!" Rocky said.

"And the hot air that makes the balloon rise comes from a gas flame," Ryder continued. "Marshall, I'll need you to make sure the heater is safe."

"I'm all fired up!" Marshall exclaimed.

The PAW Patrol raced to the town square. Rocky quickly inspected the tear in the balloon. "I've got the perfect patch in my truck," he said.

"And how do the gas tanks look?" Ryder asked.

"The big question is how do they smell," Marshall replied. He sniffed the tanks. "I don't smell any gas leaks."

Rocky glued a piece of Zuma's old surf kite over the hole.
"Good work!" Ryder exclaimed. "That patch is a perfect fit."
Ryder turned a lever and the balloon slowly filled with hot
air. The other balloons were gathering on the horizon. The
race was about to begin.

"Time to get over my fear of heights!" the mayor
shouted. "I'm going to win this race!"
 She pumped her fist and accidentally hit the lever
on the heater, flipping it all the way open. The balloon
started to fly away!

Marshall chased after the balloon. He jumped and grabbed a rope with his teeth. But the balloon didn't stop. Instead, Marshall was pulled higher and higher into the air.

Suddenly, the rope slid from Marshall's mouth and he fell!

Marshall landed right in Ryder's arms. "Thanks, Ryder!" he barked.

The race had started, and there was no time to waste. Ryder called Skye on his PupPad.

"Mayor Goodway took off without me! I need you to fly me to her balloon in your copter."

Skye slid into her Pup House, which quickly turned into a helicopter. "Let's take to the sky!" she exclaimed as she zoomed into the air.

Skye flew to Ryder and dropped a harness down to him.
He locked himself in, and Skye whisked him away.
"I'll swing you over to the balloon," Skye said. But she
had to hurry because the balloon was headed straight
for the lighthouse on Seal Island!

Ryder sailed through the air, reached out, and caught the basket!

Mayor Goodway helped Ryder climb into the balloon. He quickly gave it a burst of hot air and it rose over the lighthouse.

"Made it, Skye," Ryder reported as he undid his harness.

"Roger that!" Skye said, flying away. "Go win that trophy!"

"All right, Mayor Goodway, are you ready to win this race?"
The mayor gave Ryder a thumbs-up. "I'm in it to win it!"
They raced after the other balloons.

With Ryder at the controls, the balloon quickly caught up with Mayor Humdinger, who was in the lead.

"The race is on!" Ryder yelled.

"I've never lost a race, and I'm not starting now!" Mayor Humdinger shouted back.

With a rush of hot air, Ryder and Mayor Goodway's
balloon whooshed past Mayor Humdinger.
"There's Jake's Mountain!" Mayor Goodway exclaimed.
"The finish line is on the other side!"

"The winds are stronger up high," Ryder said.
"We'll have a better chance of winning if we go up."
"Up, up, and away!" Mayor Goodway cheered.

Ryder guided the balloon higher and rode the rushing winds over Jake's Mountain—but Mayor Humdinger did the same! His balloon zipped right past Ryder and Mayor Goodway.

Down on the ground, all the PAW Patrol pups cheered as the balloons came into view. Mayor Humdinger's balloon swooped out of the sky first . . . but Mayor Goodway and Ryder dropped ahead of him at the last second and crossed the finish line. They won the race!

Mayor Humdinger sadly handed the trophy to Mayor Goodway. "I believe this belongs to you."

Mayor Goodway gave the trophy to Ryder.
"This belongs to Ryder and the PAW Patrol."
"Thanks, Mayor Goodway!" Ryder said with a smile.
"Whenever you need a hand, just yelp for help!"

Late one afternoon, Skye was flying high over the Lookout. She was really excited because her hero, stunt pilot Ace Sorensen, was coming to the air show in Adventure Bay. Skye spun and spiraled and zipped and dipped.

"Trick flying is the best!" she exclaimed.

Down on the ground, Marshall wasn't sure he agreed. The only thing he liked to fly was his kite.

Suddenly, a big gust of wind caught Marshall's kite and blew him into the air. He got tangled in the kite's string and came crashing down—right on top of Rocky!

"Sorry," Marshall said with a grin. "I guess my landing was a little rocky."

Just then, Ryder got a call on his PupPad. It was Ace Sorensen, the stunt pilot! Her plane was having engine trouble, and she needed the PAW Patrol's help finding a place to land.

"We're on it!" Ryder declared. "No job is too big, no pup is too small!"

Ryder quickly called the pups to the Lookout
and told them about Ace. He needed Skye's
helicopter and her night-vision goggles.

"This pup's got to fly!" Skye yelped. She was
eager to help her hero.

Ryder also needed Chase's spotlight and traffic cones to make a runway at Farmer Yumi's Farm.

"Chase is on the case!" barked the eager German shepherd.

Finally, Ryder asked Rocky to fix Ace's plane.

"Green means go!" Rocky cheered.

The sun was setting as Skye zoomed through the clouds in her helicopter. She scanned the darkening sky with her goggles and spotted something in the distance. "There she is now!"

Ace's damaged plane flew past a mountain and sputtered over the treetops. Black smoke poured out of the engine, making it even harder for Ace to see.

Skye pulled ahead of Ace's plane. "Follow me!" she called, and led the way to Farmer Yumi's Farm.

Meanwhile, at the farm, Ryder, Chase, and Rocky were preparing a runway so Ace could land. Chase set up his orange safety cones to mark off the landing strip.

"Great job!" Ryder said. As the sky continued to darken, he turned to Rocky and asked if he had any old flashlights in his truck.

"I've got a bunch," Rocky replied. He quickly collected the flashlights. Then he and Ryder taped them to the traffic cones.

When they were done, Ryder called Skye and told her to watch for the runway lights.

"Roger that!" said Skye.

Skye zoomed through the starry night and spotted the glowing landing strip just over a hill. When she and Ace started to descend, there was a loud BOOM! The plane began to shake as sparks sizzled along the wing. Ace radioed to the team that she would have to parachute out of the plane!

55

Ryder didn't think parachuting in the dark was a good idea. He had another plan. "Ace, have you ever done the wing-walking stunt?" he asked.

"Ace is the greatest wing-walker in the whole world," Skye reported.

"Awesome!" Ryder exclaimed. He told Skye to lower her towline and safety harness.

Ace unbuckled her seat belt and carefully climbed onto the wing of her bouncing, shaking plane. Skye lowered her towline and harness and zoomed up close to Ace. The stunt pilot reached for the harness—but couldn't quite get it!

"I've got my parachute," Ace called. "I'm going to jump!"

"No!" Skye called back. "We can do this, Ace!"
Skye lowered her helicopter and flew in as close as she could. Ace tried again . . . and grabbed the harness! She snapped herself in and was carried through the air to Farmer Yumi's Farm.

As Skye approached the farm, Ace radioed Ryder and asked him to track someone named Amelia.

"Sure," Ryder said. "But who's Amelia?"

"My plane," Ace replied. "Every great pilot names her plane."

Ryder tracked the plane on his PupPad and saw that it was heading for a water landing in the bay!

"Let's find the plane and get it onto the beach before it sinks!" said Ryder.

Ryder and Chase raced to the bay, and Skye gently set Ace down at the farm. The stunt pilot unfastened the harness and waved up to the helicopter. "Thanks, Skye!" she called.

"No problem, Ace!" the pilot pup called back. Then she whispered excitedly to herself, "I can't believe I saved my hero!"

Splash! Amelia sputtered, then glided to a stop in the bay. Ryder sped out to the plane on his Jet Ski and hooked a cable to it. When Ryder gave the command, Chase turned on his winch and pulled *Amelia* to shore.

But when Ace saw her plane, she wasn't very hopeful about flying it in the air show. There was so much damage, she thought she'd need an entire team of mechanics to fix it all.

Luckily, she had the PAW Patrol!

"Reporting for duty," Rocky said.

63

By the glow of Chase's spotlight, Rocky riveted a patch onto Amelia's wing. At the same time, Ryder fixed the cockpit, while Ace adjusted the engine. In no time, Skye started up the plane. The propeller began to spin, and the engine roared. The plane was as good as new!

"I can't wait for the air show tomorrow," Skye said.

Ace hopped onto one of the wings. "How would you like to see my wing-walk-and-roll trick up close and personal?"

Skye thought that sounded great!

The next day was sunny and warm, and the PAW Patrol watched the air show from Adventure Bay's beach. They cheered and waved as *Amelia* flew into view. Ace climbed out of the cockpit and stood on a wing. Then the plane tilted slightly, and they saw Skye smiling behind the controls.

Suddenly, Ace jumped into the air, and Skye made the plane twirl around. When the plane was level again, Ace landed back on the wing. Ryder and the pups couldn't believe their eyes. The wing-walk-and-roll trick was the most amazing stunt they'd ever seen!

"Wow!" Rocky gasped, watching Skye zoom through the clouds. "She's so good!"

"You're all good pups," Ryder said.

The pups cheered and barked for each other as Skye and Ace zipped overhead.

When someone calls for help, the PAW Patrol race into action on their awesome vehicles.

"We can all ride in the PAW Patroller," Ryder says. "When we need to go on a rescue outside Adventure Bay, this big eighteen-wheeler can take the whole team—and our vehicles, too!

"For rescues closer to home, I hop on my speedy ATV," he explains. "At the touch of a button, it can change into a snowmobile or a Jet Ski!"

CHASE
IS ON THE
CASE!

"If you see these lights flashing and hear sirens blaring, you know I'm on the case in my police truck," says Chase. "The back has lots of room to store equipment, like orange safety cones, and the front has a winch for moving and towing big things."

 Chase's truck can also turn into a spy mobile for super-spy missions!

Marshall's fire truck can turn into an ambulance when he needs to roll out on a medical rescue!

"You're in good paws when I roll to the rescue," barks Marshall. "My fire truck is prepared for every emergency. It has hoses and water pumps to put out fires, and ladders to reach high places."

"I'm always ready to fly," says Skye.
"To take to the skies, I use my Pup Pack, with its pop-out wings! But if I'm traveling long distances, I need my helicopter."

Skye's high-flying helicopter has a claw to pick things up and a towline to carry special cargo.

 Zuma uses his submarine's claw to move really big objects.

"My hovercraft is a speedy machine on land and water," says Zuma. "It can sail over waves and launch life rings to those who need help.

"And with the press of a button, the craft becomes a submarine!"

RUBBLE ON THE DOUBLE

"If the PAW Patrol needs some heavy lifting, I'm Rubble on the double with my bulldozer," barks Rubble.

Rubble's Digger has a giant shovel on the front to move dirt, and a powerful drill on the back.

With the bits and pieces he's saved in his truck, Rocky can fix everything from ladders to windmills.

"Don't lose it—reuse it!" says Rocky. "My recycling truck is perfect for that. The forklift on the front can pick up heavy loads. And the storage area in the back is where I keep my recycling."

"Winter rescues are no problem for me and my snowcat," barks Everest. "These heavy-duty treads get me over icy hills, and the plow can clear any snowy road."

If there's a really big obstacle in the way, like a fallen tree, Everest's plow has a claw that can pick it up and move it!

On land, in the air, or under the
water, the PAW Patrol are always
ready to lend a paw. Just yelp for
help, and they'll be on the roll!